What do two little penguins do?

A book of months

WHAT DO TWO LITTLE PENGUINS DO?
A BOOK OF MONTHS

Published in 2006 in the U.S.A. by Dalmatian Press, LLC.

Illustrator: *Dona Gelsinger*
Writer: *Kathyrn Knight*
Designer: *Tatia M. Lockridge*

ISBN: 1-40373-261-2
15861/0906

Printed in the U.S.A.

06 07 08 09 LBM 10 9 8 7 6 5 4 3 2 1

What do two little penguins do?

A book of months

Illustrated by Dona Gelsinger

Written by Kathryn Knight

Dalmatian Press

Far, far away . . .

...where cold winds swirl
'round frosty lands of the Southern Pole,
two little penguins have a wonderful time
all year long.

And just what *do* those
two little penguins do?

In January…

…while you're curled up with hot cocoa,
listening to a delightful fairy tale…

What do two little penguins do?

They slip and slide,
and jump and glide,
then wiggle and giggle
on a snowman ride!

That's what two little penguins do!

In February…

…while you make Valentines
with paper hearts and glitter and glue
and lovely touches of color…

What do two little penguins do?

They say, “I love you,”
penguin style
with an Eskimo kiss
and a warm, silly smile.

That’s what two little penguins do!

In March…

…while you skip outdoors to fly a kite
on a gust of wind
on a blustery day…

What do two little penguins do?

They catch the breeze
and fly with ease
across the snow
with *Yay*'s and
Wheeeeeeeeeeeeee's!

That's what two little penguins do!

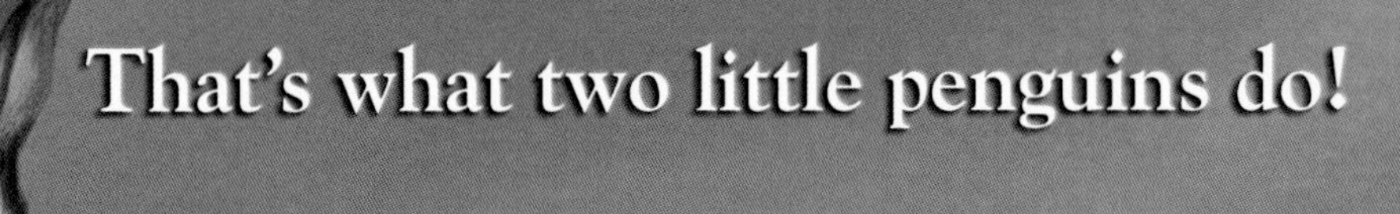

In April...

...while you happily gather blooming buds
and flowers for
a Spring bouquet...

What do two little penguins do?

They gather snowballs
for Spring flinging!
There's laughter after *splats*!—
and singing!

That's what two little penguins do!

In May...

...while you treat Mom to breakfast in bed,
and handmade gifts,
and plenty of kisses...

What do two little penguins do?

They snuggle up close
for homespun fun,
with tickles and hugs
for everyone.

That's what two little penguins do!

In June...

...while you swing on a branch,
or wriggle your toes in a pebbly brook,
or count the stars on a moonless night...

What do two little penguins do?

They *swi-n-n-ng*
and rock and roll
while they
have a frolicky time
on a jolly-cold day.

That's what two little penguins do!

In July…

…while you "ooooh" and "aaaah"
as brilliant hues light up the sky
on the 4th of July…

What do two little penguins do?

They watch in wonder,
eyes aglow,
the grand aurora!
My! What a show!

That's what two little penguins do!

In August...

...while you scoop sand
on a warm, sunny shore,
or hum in a hammock the livelong day...

What do two little penguins do?

They just pretend it's hot
(it's not!)
and find a "cool"
vacation spot!

That's what two little penguins do!

In September...

...while you skip off to school to learn
your ABCs and 123s...

What do two little penguins do?

They play with schools of fish
and learn
some slippery, flippery games
in turn!

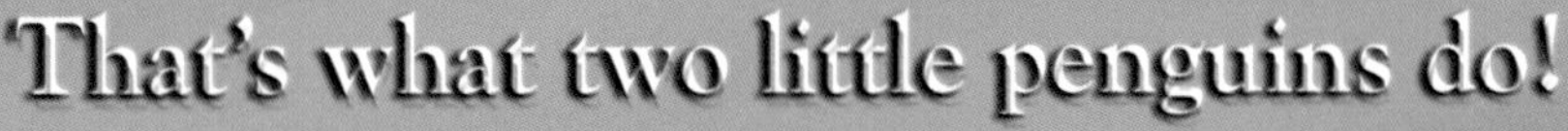

That's what two little penguins do!

In October…

…while you carve pumpkins
and plan with friends
to trick-or-treat on Halloween…

What do two little penguins do?

They huddle and cuddle
on a clear, bright eve
and tell tall tales
of make-believe.

That's what two little penguins do!

In November…

…while you help snap the long green beans
and mash the potatoes
for a day of feasting…

What do two little penguins do?

They fill their rumbly tummies,
then…
have a slip-n-tumble time
with a roly-poly friend.

That's what two little penguins do!

In December…

…while you wrap gifts and trim the tree
and sing out carols merrily…

What do two little penguins do?

They visit friends
and chirp good cheer
to celebrate
their happy year.

That's what two little penguins do!

And on Christmas Eve…

…while you watch the sky
and try to spy
a sleigh with Santa flying by…

What do two little penguins do?

Why…

…the same as you!